TO WALK THE SKY

How Iroquois Steelworkers Helped Build Towering Cities

By **Patricia Morris Buckley**

Illustrated by **E. B. Lewis**

Heartdrum

An Imprint of HarperCollinsPublishers

Heartdrum is an imprint of HarperCollins Publishers.

Library of Congress Cataloging-in-Publication Data

Names: Buckley, Patricia Morris, author. | Lewis, E. B. (Earl Bradley), 1956– illustrator.
Title: To walk the sky : how Iroquois steelworkers helped build towering cities / by
   Patricia Morris Buckley; illustrated by E.B. Lewis.
Other titles: How Iroquois steelworkers helped build towering cities.
Description: First edition. | New York, NY : Heartdrum, an imprint of HarperCollins
   Publishers, [2023] | Audience: Ages 4–8 | Audience: Grades K–1 | Summary: "Mohawk
   author Patricia Morris Buckley tells the story of the brave skywalkers—Native men
   who work as high steelworkers, building bridges and skyscrapers no matter the
   dangers"— Provided by publisher.
Identifiers: LCCN 2023037588 | ISBN 9780063046979 (hardcover)
Subjects: LCSH: Mohawk Indians—Juvenile literature. | Iroquois Indians—Juvenile
   literature. | Construction workers—Juvenile literature. | Building, Iron and steel—
   History—Juvenile literature. | Skyscrapers—History—Juvenile literature. | Pont de
   Québec (Québec)—History—Juvenile literature.
Classification: LCC E99.M8 B74 2024 | DDC 624.08997071—dc23/eng/20231024
LC record available at https://lccn.loc.gov/2023037588

The artist used watercolor on paper to
create the illustrations for this book.
Typography by Dana Fritts
24 25 26 27 28 RTLO 10 9 8 7 6 5 4 3 2 1

First Edition

For my father, Richard D. Morris,
who taught me the importance of our Mohawk history
and to be proud of our rich Native roots

–P.M.B.

To the victims of 9/11 and their families

–E.B.L.

Look to the sky! Far, far up you might spy Native American skywalkers as they balance on narrow steel beams among the clouds.

Skywalkers were born in the days of great-great-grandfathers, when Mohawks from eastern Canada's Caughnawaga reserve picked up hammers and a handful of rivets to tread steel girders high above. Calm and sure-footed, skywalkers living near the St. Lawrence River walked the narrow beams as if strolling down a sidewalk.

More than a hundred years ago, Caughnawaga's boundaries preserved the traditions of Mohawk life but also kept residents from better-paying jobs. Beyond the reserve's borders, no one hired Native Americans. Families went hungry, hands were idle, and hearts dreamed of building something other than the longhouses where their ancestors once dwelled.

The Dominion Bridge Company asked for some reserve land to begin a railway bridge over the river to Montreal. Tribal elders agreed on one condition: Caughnawagans would be given jobs.

Construction bosses used Mohawks for unskilled labor and forbade them from climbing the uncompleted bridge. But when French Canadian workers went home for the day, Mohawks scaled the bridge to walk and run on the beams as if they were giant tightropes. How these daredevils thrilled at being so high. One false step could lead to a horrific fall!

The bosses called them skywalkers, astonished by the Mohawks' steadfast balance, and finally let them work atop the bridge. Masking any fear of heights, the Native men found that skywalking came naturally to them. They also learned that joining pieces of iron with rivets paid them more than hauling stones— much more. Soon they were the ones uniting girders and, with the higher wages, making sure their families had full bellies. Most of all, they took great pride in creating a legacy of landmarks that would outlive them.

When the railroad decided to build a bridge across the St. Lawrence River near Quebec City to the north, thirty-eight skywalkers from Caughnawaga were hired to help construct an engineering wonder—the longest bridge of its kind in the world.

They worked one year, two, then three, as the bridge stretched from the river's south side toward the north. That's when the creaks and groans began. High in the structure, skywalkers felt the girders sway. They whispered their fears in Mohawk, even after the boss said not to worry.

On a hot afternoon in August 1907, just before the end-of-day whistle, ironworkers gathering their tools felt the beams bend under their feet.

Seconds later, the entire bridge shook, then screamed. Nineteen thousand tons of steel twisted, crashing into the rushing, unforgiving waters below, taking eighty-six men down with it. From miles away, its impact felt like an earthquake. After the crashing stopped, all that could be heard were the wails of French Canadian wives waiting on the shore to walk their men home.

More than a two-hour drive away, frantic Native families gathered around the only telephone on the reserve.

Waiting and praying. Praying and waiting. Through tears, they learned that seventy-five of the eighty-six ironworkers on the bridge were gone forever—thirty-three of them from Caughnawaga. Almost every tribal family lost a skywalker. In one family, all four sons perished.

Grieving metalworkers crafted grave markers from iron that had crashed into the river. They also constructed two giant steel crosses that acted as twin sentries at opposite ends of the reserve.

Yet skywalking remained the best way to feed their families and keep them warm during hard winters. Tragedy would not keep the men from their place in the sky. So, clan mothers, who decided what was best for the whole tribe, ruled that all the men in one family could not work on the same project. Never again would nearly an entire generation of men disappear in one horrible moment.

Caughnawagan men scattered to cities all over North America. Their first project in New York City was the Hell Gate Bridge in 1916.

They sat with their feet dangling in thirty-five stories of air, eating lunch with the best views in the world. Generation after generation, skywalkers sculpted city skylines that pierced the clouds.

During the 1920s, a New York City housing boom led the men from the neighboring Mohawk reserve of Akwesasne to take up skywalking. Over the years, the Six Nations of the Iroquois Confederacy, plus the Algonquins, joined them on the high beams, although Mohawks still outnumbered other Native Nations. The accomplishments and reputations of Native American ironworkers spread throughout North America.

They were best known for working on the Twin
Towers of New York City's World Trade Center,
then the tallest buildings in the world. Skywalkers
showed pride in their contribution by signing the
last beam before connecting it to the South Tower.

On September 11, 2001, planes piloted by terrorists hit the Twin Towers, causing them to collapse to the cruel ground below. Skywalkers volunteered to dismantle what their fathers and uncles had built decades before. They understood all too well how mangled beams broke hearts.

Once again, Native ironworkers would not let tragedy defeat them. They were among the steelworkers who attached a spire atop One World Trade Center, where the towers once stood. The spire antenna made the building the tallest in the Western Hemisphere at the time.

A few years later, all the people of Eastern Canada, including First Nations citizens, commemorated the hundredth anniversary of the Quebec Bridge disaster. Back on the reserve (now called Kahnawà:ke), Mohawk volunteers built a steel replica of a section of the original bridge. Families of the perished men planted young English oak trees around the memorial, one for each skywalker lost.

As those trees grew, they stretched their branches to the sky—reminding people of the generations of skywalkers who had strolled among the clouds and even dared to touch the heavens.

And in cities across the continent, skywalkers continue to build towering structures, just like their great-great-grandfathers. Today, they work in places such as Detroit, New York City, and Vancouver. Native women, too, have entered the profession, building a future on steel beams high in the air.

Look up! Can you see them? These are the courageous Native Americans who, even today, walk the sky.

THE STORY OF MY FAMILY

One hundred years after the Quebec Bridge's collapse, when Kahnawà:ke commemorated the skywalkers who had died, my family was among those who planted a tree in remembrance.

My great-grandfather John Charles "Tehoronhiate" Morris perished that fateful day in 1907. Nine-year-old John Roy Morris, my grandfather, lost his father. And Frank, my grandfather's unborn baby brother, never even met his father.

My great-grandfather's death had major repercussions on our family. My grandfather's mother begged her sons not to follow the path of a skywalker. Yet our family's history with building continued. My grandfather became a machinist, crafting metal, and eventually left the reserve. As a mechanical engineer, my father designed parts for airplanes. And I, with my head always in the clouds, became a builder of stories.

One of many volunteers, my father helped build the bridge memorial on the reserve for the hundredth anniversary of the tragedy. My eldest uncle, John Morris Jr., planted our family's tree as the bells rang all over Eastern Canada. The branches of our Native family tree continue to grow and flourish.

While we no longer live on the banks of the mighty St. Lawrence River, we still honor the memories and ways of our ancestors, passing them from one generation to the next.

THE STORY OF THE QUEBEC BRIDGE

As trains sped over the newly built Montreal Bridge (officially known as the Victoria Bridge) in 1859, the leaders of the city of Quebec, approximately 150 miles away, could imagine the advantages of speeding up trade and not having to shut down due to the river being blocked by ice for four months every year. It took decades of fundraising, during which many architects vied for the honor of designing the bridge. One contender was Alexandre-Gustave Eiffel, well-known for designing bridges long before he created the Eiffel Tower and the scaffolding for the Statue of Liberty.

But the Quebec Bridge Company gave the job to Theodore Cooper, a well-known bridge architect, who had never designed a bridge this long. Cooper decided not only on a cantilever design, with no posts in the middle of the bridge, but on one with the longest cantilever ever built. The center section spanned 1,800 feet, which meant ships could pass under it in the river's center, the deepest part of the waterway.

Unfortunately, ill health kept Cooper from overseeing the construction firsthand. When beams showed signs of twisting, and rivet holes didn't match, he was more than four hundred miles away in New York City during an era when most communication happened by mail. He refused to have a government inspector on site, claiming that he wanted the final word on every technical decision. His choice proved catastrophic. After the bridge crashed into the river, a special commission determined that too much weight had been put on the cantilever section, which caused the bridge to collapse.

Cooper retired, never to build a bridge again.

A few years later, Quebec officials revived the idea of a bridge. They decided to use the original design with modifications. This time, the middle section was floated out to the center and raised into place. Just before it was attached to the iron framework, the center section slipped into the river, killing thirteen men (none of them skywalkers).

It wasn't until 1917 that Quebec finally had its bridge. It is still the longest cantilever bridge in the world.

In 2007, I walked the bridge as the wind twisted my hair into tangles. I wondered if my great-grandfather felt the same as he worked high in the girders of that first bridge. Down below, I could just spy twisted metal under the water's surface. In that moment I felt connected to my family's past in a deeper way than I ever had before.

THE STORY OF KAHNAWÀ:KE

*T*he Mohawk world before Europeans arrived in North America was filled with conflict. The Five Nations of the Iroquois were constantly at war with one another until the Great Peacemaker, a man sent by the Creator to bring peace to the Iroquois, and the legendary Onondagan chief, Hiawatha, helped create a union called the Iroquois Confederacy.

Mohawk land stretched from the Mohawk Valley in what we now call New York State to just north of what is now known as the Canadian border. (Mohawks are the Keepers of the Eastern Door, as they live on the eastern side of Iroquois land.) We Mohawk people were sustained by planting the "three sisters"—corn, squash, and beans—and by harvesting a wide variety of wild plants. The men also trapped, fished, and hunted wild animals for food. Multiple families of a clan lived in shared longhouses.

Clan mothers selected the male leaders of our tribes. The men made the decisions, which the women oversaw. If the clan mothers disagreed with the men's choices, they would remove the leaders from their positions. This balance kept order and continuity in our community.

When Europeans arrived, along with their cash economy, Mohawk men started to sell or trade them animal furs.

Kahnawà:ke reserve (first called Caughnawaga) was created by French Canadian Jesuit missionaries for Native people who had converted to Catholicism in the 1700s. While most of our reserve residents are Mohawk, there are other Native nations represented as well. Kahnawà:ke residents are known as Kahnawakero:non. Kahnawà:ke means "place of the rapids," referring to living on the banks of the swiftly moving St. Lawrence River.

Present-day Kahnawà:ke is roughly nineteen miles square and is home to approximately eight thousand people. It lies across the river from Montreal. It was also the home of the only First Nations saint, Kateri Tekakwitha, canonized by the Catholic Church in 2012.

Many of the skywalkers from Kahnawà:ke moved to New York City in the early 1920s—creating a neighborhood in Brooklyn called Little Caughnawaga, or North Gowanus—rather than making the four-hundred-mile trek every week.

In the beginning, First Nations people crossing from Canada to New York for work were challenged by border agencies. In 1926, a lawsuit brought in the name of skywalker Paul Diabo won the right for Native Americans to cross the border freely, citing the Jay Treaty of 1794, which allowed our Native people to travel to tribal lands that countries had divided with their borders.

The construction of Interstate 87, which started in 1957 and took more than ten years, cut the commute to six hours. Many skywalkers then moved their families back to the reserve, commuting home on weekends.

Today the residents of Kahnawà:ke live a rich life that centers on family, traditions, and community. The Native American sport of lacrosse is still played by many. In the winter, snow snakes (long, greased, spear-tipped wooden poles) slither down hills to the thrill of Mohawks young and old.

Kahnawà:ke people no longer live in longhouses, preferring single-family homes. But there's a fervor to keep the Mohawk culture thriving in our community. For instance, the Mohawk language returned to the community in the late 1900s when schools began to teach the Mohawk tongue. Powwow festivals teach Native traditions to each new generation. And once again, the reserve rings with the sounds of people of all ages enjoying lives in ways that would make their ancestors proud.

GLOSSARY

beam—A long, narrow piece of building material that holds weight and construction.

cantilever bridge—A bridge in which the middle section is counterbalanced by structures near the shore.

First Nations—Native Americans who live in Canada.

Iroquois Confederacy—Originally made up of the Five Nations: Mohawk, Cayuga, Onondaga, Oneida, and Seneca. Later, the Tuscarora people were admitted, making it the Six Nations.

powwow—A Native American event with traditional singing, dancing, and food.

reserve—In Canada, First Nations reservations are called reserves, which have their own laws, leaders, and governing systems.

rivet—A metal pin that looks like a thick nail. It goes through the holes in two pieces of material, then is flattened on the no-head side to anchor the two pieces together.

September 11, 2001—On this date, terrorists hijacked four US airplanes with the intent to crash into and destroy four targets. Two of the planes flew into the World Trade Center's Twin Towers. Both structures collapsed, taking the lives of more than 2,500 people. Today, a memorial stands on the site where the towers once rose 110 stories into the air.

A SAMPLE OF BUILDINGS CONSTRUCTED BY SKYWALKERS

The Iroquois have left their mark on many structures, including the George Washington Bridge, the Empire State Building, Rockefeller Center, the Deutsche Bank Center, the Chrysler Building, the headquarters of the United Nations, the Woolworth Building, the Seagram Building, Lincoln Center, the Verrazzano-Narrows Bridge, and the Waldorf Astoria, all in New York City. They also worked on San Francisco's Golden Gate Bridge, Chicago's Sears Tower, and Vancouver's Lions Gate Bridge, among countless other projects.

The tradition continues today. Recent projects include an Amazon facility in Syracuse, New York; Cornell University dormitories in Ithaca, New York; a Chrysler plant in Detroit, Michigan; Yankee Stadium in the Bronx, New York; a facility for the Fire Department of New York in Brooklyn, New York; and numerous schools and hospitals.

ACKNOWLEDGMENTS

The author would like to thank two museum curators who assisted with additional research: Colette Lemmon, curator of exhibitions for the Iroquois Museum's exhibit *Walking the Steel: From Girder to Ground Zero*, and Devorah Romanek, assistant curator for the Smithsonian's National Museum of the American Indian's exhibit *Booming Out: Mohawk Ironworkers Build New York*. Niá:wen. Thanks also to Elders Eddie "Two Axe" Martin and Teiowí:sonte Thomas Deer of the Kanien'kehá:ka Onkwawén:na Raotitióhkwa Language and Cultural Center.

A NOTE FROM CYNTHIA LEITICH SMITH, AUTHOR-CURATOR OF HEARTDRUM

Dear Reader,

If you peer up from a sidewalk, the Caughnawagan ironworkers seem larger than life. After all, they play a big role in raising mighty cities where millions live and work and go to school. They build bridges to support countless travelers across immense bodies of water.

They're also everyday people, Mohawk people. They are dads and uncles, brothers and cousins. They have families who love them and pray for their safety. They deserve our respect and our thanks.

What I admire most about the skywalkers is the way they face challenges—even heartbreaking loss—and find the strength to mourn, heal, and carry on. Even if you're not an ironworker, you'll face challenges. We all do. Like me, you may want to look to their example for inspiration.

This picture book is published by Heartdrum, a Native-focused imprint of HarperCollins Children's Books, which highlights stories about Native heroes by Indigenous authors and illustrators. I'm honored that this book is on our list. The fact that the author is from a family of ironworkers comes through in her precise attention to factual detail and the emotional truths she has woven into the text. The illustrator's artwork lifts us up to the day-to-day life of skywalkers and shines a light on their soaring story.

Mvto,
Cynthia Leitich Smith

In 2014, We Need Diverse Books (WNDB) began as a simple hashtag on Twitter. The social media campaign soon grew into a 501(c)(3) nonprofit with a team that spans the globe. WNDB is supported by a network of writers, illustrators, agents, editors, teachers, librarians, and book lovers, all united under the same goal—to create a world where every child can see themselves in the pages of a book. You can learn more about WNDB programs at www.diversebooks.org.